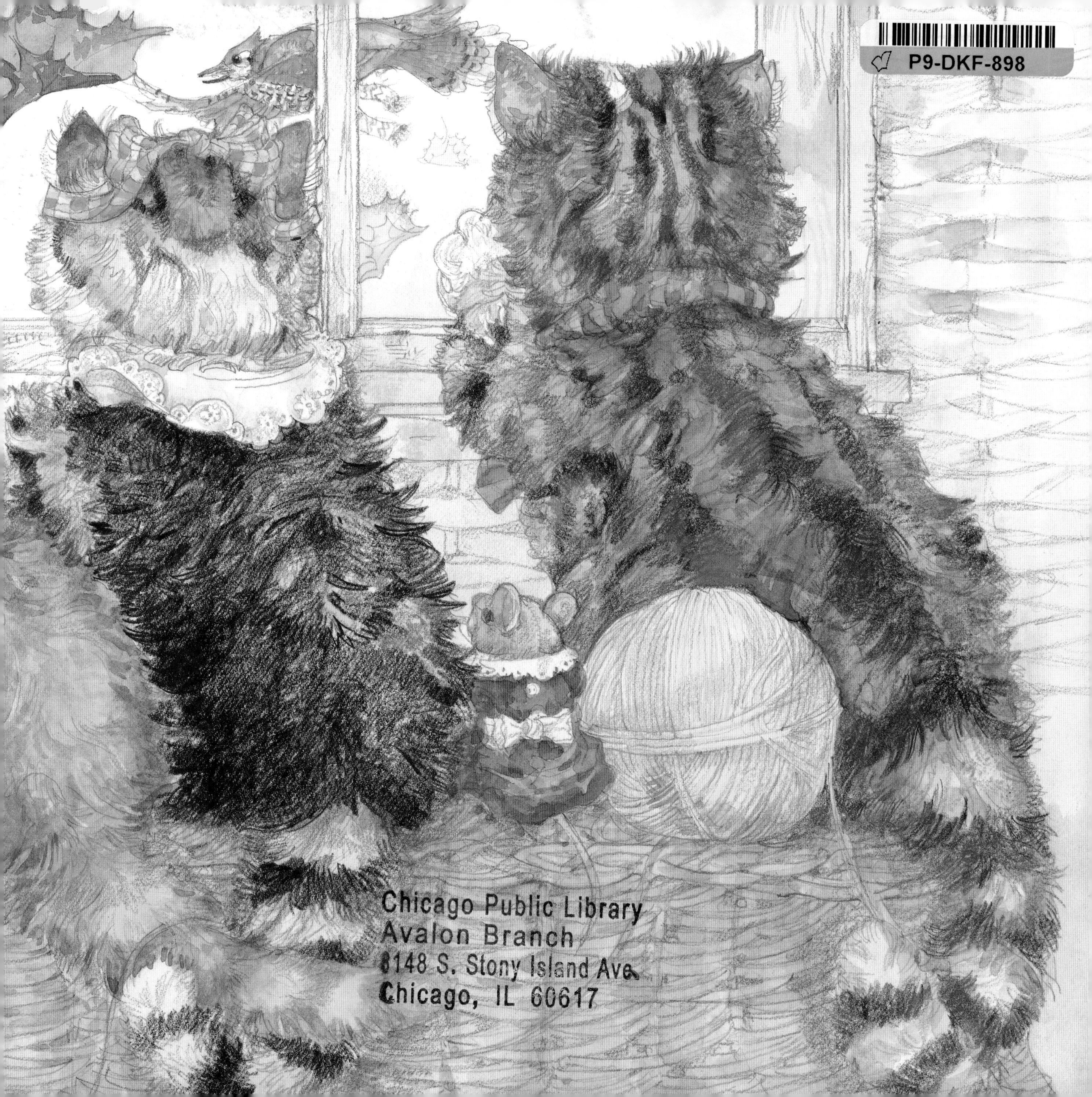

Three Little Kittens

JERRY PINKNEY

Dial Books for Young Readers

an imprint of Penguin Group (USA) Inc.

DIAL BOOKS FOR YOUNG READERS

A division of Penguin Young Readers Group • Published by The Penguin Group • Penguin Group (USA) Inc., 375 Hudson Street, New York, NY 10014, U.S.A. • Penguin Group (Canada), 90 Eglinton Avenue East, Suite 700, Toronto, Ontario, Canada M4P 2Y3 (a division of Pearson Penguin Canada Inc.) • Penguin Books Ltd, 80 Strand, London WC2R 0RL, England • Penguin Ireland, 25 St. Stephen's Green, Dublin 2, Ireland (a division of Penguin Books Ltd) • Penguin Group (Australia), 250 Camberwell Road, Camberwell, Victoria 3124, Australia (a division of Pearson Australia Group Pty Ltd) • Penguin Books India Pvt Ltd, 11 Community Centre, Panchsheel Park, New Delhi - 110 017, India • Penguin Group (NZ), 67 Apollo Drive, Rosedale, North Shore 0632, New Zealand (a division of Pearson New Zealand Ltd) • Penguin Books (South Africa) (Pty) Ltd, 24 Sturdee Avenue, Rosebank, Johannesburg 2196, South Africa • Penguin Books Ltd, Registered Offices: 80 Strand, London WC2R 0RL, England

Designed by Lily Malcom • Text set in ITC Stone Informal • Music composition by Bob Sherwin • Manufactured in China on acid-free paper
10 9 8 7 6 5 4 3 2 1

Library of Congress Cataloging-in-Publication Data
Pinkney, Jerry.
Three little kittens / Jerry Pinkney.   p. cm.
Summary: Presents the classic tale of three youngsters who are careless with their mittens, but who turn out to be good little kittens after all.
ISBN 978-0-8037-3533-0 (hardcover)   1. Nursery rhymes. 2. Children's poetry. [1. Nursery rhymes.] I. Title. PZ8.3.P55868312Thr 2010
398.8—dc22   [E]   2009051660

The full-color artwork was prepared using graphite, color pencil, and watercolor.

Readers: Be sure to look on the underside of the book jacket for the "Three Little Kittens" song.

To my publisher Lauri; her daughter, Ruby; and their cat, Sushi. meow, meow, meow

Three little kittens,
They got new mittens
And they began to cheer.
"Oh mother dear, oh mother dear,
May we go out to play?"

"Put on your mittens,
You sweet little kittens,
And you may go and play.
meow, meow, meow
Yes, you may go and play."

The three little kittens,
They played and played.

They spun and leaped
and pounced.

"Oh mother dear, we sadly fear,
Our mittens we have lost!"

"What! Lost your mittens?
    You careless kittens.
    Then you shall have no pie!"

Meow, meow, the kittens cried,
    For they would have no pie.

"Let's find our mittens!"
    then said the kittens.
    meow, meow, meow

Soon one little kitten had found her mittens!
purr, purr, purr

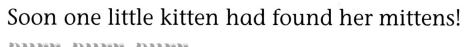

Then the second kitten had found his mittens!
purr, purr, purr

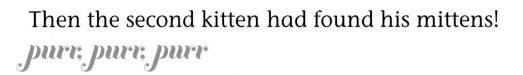

And the third little kitten
then found his mittens!
purr, purr, purr

"Oh mother dear, see here, see here!
Our mittens we have found."

"What! Found your mittens?
You darling kittens.
Now you shall have some pie.
meow, meow, meow
You shall have some pie."

purr, purr, purr, purr
They soon ate up the pie.

"Oh mother dear, look here, look here!
  We fear we've made a mess."

"You silly kittens,
   You're wearing your mittens!"
Their mother began to sigh.
meow, meow, meow
They all began to sigh.

The three little kittens,
They washed their mittens . . .

And hung them out to dry.

"Oh mother dear, see here, see here!
  Our mittens we have washed."
"What! Washed your mittens?
  My good little kittens."
meow, meow, meow

The three little kittens
Put on the clean mittens
And they began to cheer.
"Oh mother dear, oh mother dear,
May we go out to play?"